Rocky

Saddle Up Series
Book 51

Dave and Pat Sargent are longtime residents of Prairie Grove, Arkansas. Dave, a fourth-generation dairy farmer, began writing in early December 1990. Pat, a former teacher, began writing in the fourth grade. They enjoy the outdoors and have a real love for animals.

Rocky

Saddle Up Series
Book 51

By Dave and Pat Sargent

Beyond "The End"
By Sue Rogers

Illustrated by Jane Lenoir

Ozark Publishing, Inc.
P.O. Box 228
Prairie Grove, AR 72753

Cataloging-in-Publication Data

Sargent, Dave, 1941–
    Rocky / by Dave and Pat Sargent ;
illustrated by Jane Lenoir.—Prairie Grove, AR :
Ozark Publishing, c2004.
    p. cm. (Saddle up series ; 51)

    "Be free"—Cover.
    SUMMARY: Rocky, a palomino horse,
helps hide the Liberty Bell in a safe place.
Contains factual information about blue-eyed
palomino horses.
    ISBN 1-56763-713-2 (hc)
        1-56763-714-0 (pbk)

    1. Horses—Juvenile fiction. [1. Horses—
Juvenile fiction. 2. Horses—Fiction. 3. Liberty
Bell—Fiction.] I. Sargent, Pat, 1936–
II. Lenoir, Jane, 1950– ill. III. Title. IV. Series.

    PZ10.3.S243Rl 2004
    [Fic]—dc21   2001005627

Printed in the United States of America

iv

Inspired by

blue-eyed palomino horses we see as we visit schools across the country.

Dedicated to

kids with blue eyes
and golden hair.

Foreword

Rocky is a blue-eyed palomino with a golden coat of hair. A man chooses Rocky to help with a special job. They head for Philadelphia, where Rocky's job is to help save the Liberty Bell from being stolen and melted down by the British.

Contents

If you would like to have the authors of the Saddle Up Series visit your school, free of charge, call 1-800-321-5671 or 1-800-960-3876.

One

The Blue-Eyed Palomino

The Rocking S Horse Ranch was quiet. "Too quiet!" Rocky the blue-eyed palomino thought as he paced back and forth in the corral. "This is so boring."

"I just wish," he said in a loud nicker, "that something exciting would happen around here."

His voice sounded like thunder against the stillness of the afternoon. His horse friends had been dozing peacefully, but the unexpected noise aroused them from pleasant dreams.

Rocky felt embarrassed as they all stared at him.

"Sorry, guys," he mumbled. "But I really am bored. Let's play some games or tell each other tall tales or something."

The slate grullo shook his head and said, "Rocky, it feels good to relax for a change. Just try to enjoy this calm afternoon."

"Yuk!" the blue-eyed palomino snorted. "You all go back to sleep. I'm going to find something fun to do."

A moment later, he jumped the corral fence. With ears alert and head high, he scanned the country-side for any sign of excitement. Suddenly he heard a nicker in the distance. He saw a horse and buggy coming down the road. The rig was moving so fast that dust billowed from beneath the wheels.

"Hi, stranger," Rocky yelled to the buggy horse. "Welcome to the Rocking S Horse Ranch."

"Thanks," the silver dun gasped as he loped toward the main head-quarters. "I'm sure ready for a rest. My boss is looking for a special horse to do a special job."

Rocky drew a deep breath. "Aha!" he thought. "This is my chance to do something exciting." He pranced proudly toward the horse and buggy, hoping the men sitting in the rig would be impressed. When they didn't look his way, he pawed the ground with one front hoof. Then he reared up on his hind legs. With clear blue eyes, he studied the very startled expressions on their faces.

"Oops," he murmured quietly. "They're impressed, all right. I should not have done that. I scared both of them!"

The blue-eyed palomino was very relieved as the ranch manager approached the strangers and said, "Welcome to the Rocking S, boys. What can we do for you?"

One of the men stepped down from the buggy and wiped his face with a handkerchief.

"We have been traveling long and hard," the stranger explained, "to find the perfect horse for a very important job."

The ranch manager looked at Rocky and chuckled, "Well, I see that you have met one of our best." He stroked the neck of the blue-eyed palomino as he added, "Usually Rocky is a calm, level-headed horse. I don't know why he's acting like he is. He seems anxious to get your attention."

"It's boredom, Ranch Boss," Rocky grumbled. "Just a big bunch of boredom."

"Maybe he wants the job," the man said with a sigh. Suddenly he hurried to the ranch manager with one hand extended. "Forgive my manners, sir," he said apologetically. "I am Seymore Idunno. My name is not at all important, but the safety of the Liberty Bell is of the utmost importance." Rocky nodded his head, and Seymore immediately added, "I do like the looks of this blue-eyed palomino. He may be just the right horse to save our nation's greatest symbol of freedom."

"Hmmm," the ranch manager murmured. "And just how can Rocky the blue-eyed palomino save the Liberty Bell?"

"We have reason to believe," the man continued, "that the British are going to try to steal and melt down the Liberty Bell! We do not want it to be a casualty of war."

"Oh mercy!" Rocky groaned. "We must not let them demolish our symbol of freedom." He lifted his right knee, and Seymore quickly shook it. The blue-eyed palomino smiled as his brand-new boss handed folded money to the ranch manager. Only moments later, he was trotting proudly beside the buggy horse.

"I have found my excitement, friends," he called to the horses in the corral. "I hope I see you again."

"Good luck, Rocky," replied the slate grullo.

"Be careful," the dark buckskin nickered.

"Protect the Liberty Bell for all of us, okay?" the dappled palomino neighed.

"I will protect it with my life," Rocky promised as he hit a fast trot toward Philadelphia, Pennsylvania.

Two

The Symbol of Freedom

Rocky enjoyed the trip through new country. He visited with horses along the way and was fascinated by the city of Philadelphia.

They stopped in front of the State House, which housed the Liberty Bell. Seymore said, "Okay, Rocky. This is where your work begins. Be ready to travel tonight."

"Whoa, Boss," the blue-eyed palomino whinnied. "That's what we've been doing for several days now. Can't I rest just a little while?"

He shuffled one hoof in the dirt before quietly adding, "Never mind, Boss. At least I'm not bored, right? I promise to stop complaining. Let's save that bell!"

The moon was peeking over the eastern horizon when Rocky saw Seymore hurrying toward the corral.

"Hi, Boss," he nickered loudly. "Are we ready to go to work?"

"Shhh," Boss Seymore hissed. "We have to be very quiet. There may be British spies in the area."

"Oops," Rocky whinnied. "Sorry, Boss. I'll be quiet as a little mouse." He raised his head as he added, "And brave as a lion."

An hour later, the palomino was hitched to a wagon at the back door of the State House. His ears shot forward as he listened to the men in the building grunting and groaning.

"This thing must weigh a ton!" one of the men exclaimed.

"That's very close to what it weighs, my friends," Seymore said.

"To be exact, it weighs two thousand
and eighty pounds."

As the men carried the bell toward Rocky and the wagon, the blue eyed palomino whinnied, "Be careful, men. We wouldn't want to drop it."

Seymore patted the bell with one hand.

"This symbol of freedom," he said, "could very possibly see the abolishment of slavery and the equality of all men, Rocky. If," he added sternly, "we protect it now."

A short time later, Rocky was trotting up the narrow road toward Allentown, Pennsylvania with a load of hay covering the precious cargo. Suddenly three horses and British soldiers stepped onto the road in front of him.

"Halt!" a tall lean soldier boss demanded.

Rocky glared at the linebacked dun standing in front of him.

"Just what is your problem?" he asked in a gruff tone of voice. "Is it illegal to haul hay in Great Britain?"

"You seem to be hauling hay," the dun snarled, "at a strange time of night."

"My boss is a very ambitious American," Rocky said proudly. "He works day and night."

"Humph," the dun snorted. "I feel sorry for you."

"Let the hay wagon pass," the British soldier ordered. "Anybody who's crazy enough to haul hay in the middle of the night should not be messed with."

"Thank you, sir," Seymore said with a doff of his hat. "Let's get back to work, Rocky. We'll have cows to milk soon and chickens to feed."

"Sure enough, Boss," Rocky agreed. "The British have put us a bit behind schedule."

The nation's Liberty Bell was safely hidden away underneath the floor of the Zion Reformed Church in Allentown as the sun peeked over the eastern horizon.

"Rocky," Seymore said as he stepped up on the wagon, "you are indeed the right horse for a very important job. Well done, my good friend!"

"Thanks, Boss," the palomino whinnied. "It's a real honor to help protect our symbol of freedom."

Three

The Liberty Bell

In 1778, a year after the Liberty Bell was safely hidden beneath the floor in Allentown, Rocky and Seymore returned to the Zion Reformed Church, this time to take the Liberty Bell home.

Excitement rippled through the palomino as he watched the men carefully retrieve the Liberty Bell and place it on the wagon bed.

"Wow, Boss," he said hoarsely, "we saved the bell from the British, and now we can take it home.

21

Except now," he added, "its home is called Independence Hall."

The journey to Philadelphia was good. And as they once again entered the patriotic city, folks began gathering along the streets. The Liberty Bell was not covered by hay this time. The symbol of freedom glistened beneath the rays of sun, proclaiming its presence in America.

Rocky pranced proudly amid the applause and cheers of all the onlookers. "Hmmm," he thought. "I wish my friends on the Rocking S Horse Ranch could see me now."

He heard a familiar nicker and saw the slate grullo standing in front of Independence Hall.

"Hi there, Rocky," he shouted. "You sure don't look bored now. You look proud and smug."

"I feel proud and smug," Rocky said. "Our nation is so busy that I haven't had time to be bored."

"Are folks going to ring the bell when it's unloaded and put in its proper place?" the slate grullo asked.

"No," Rocky replied. "It does not have to be loud to be heard."

As Seymore and five other men lifted the massive bell from the wagon bed, the crowd again cheered.

"I see what you mean," the grullo said with a nod of his head. "The volume and tone is not really important. What it stands for is."

"Right on, my American horse friend," Rocky said. "And this bell has just begun to speak its mind."

That evening Rocky heard the barn door open. He watched his boss Seymore quietly walk to his stall and sit down on a bale of hay.

"What's the matter, Boss?" Rocky asked. "We did a good job of protecting the Liberty Bell, didn't we?"

Seymore sat on the bale of hay with his chin resting on one hand.

"Boss," the blue-eyed palomino persisted. "What's wrong with you? Are you afraid the British will sneak back and steal it?"

There was no reply. With a worried look, Rocky stared at him for a moment. Then suddenly, the man cleared his voice to speak.

"I'm afraid," he said, "that our new nation is just beginning to fight for freedom. The Liberty Bell reminds us of the importance of independence, but we have much more to learn from its meaning."

"Every journey," the blue-eyed palomino murmured, "begins with the first step, Boss. And protecting the Liberty Bell is a giant first step."

Rocky thought for a minute, then nickered, "That is a profound statement! Folks will learn that the Liberty Bell represents both dignity and honor among all Americans. And this bell will be a shining star within history."

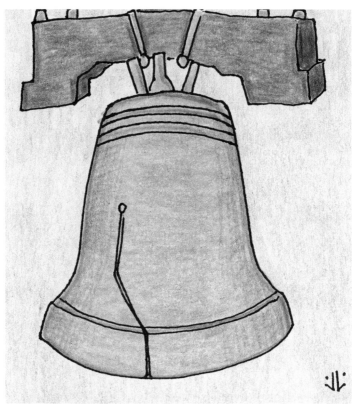

"Folks may not remember Seymore Idunno, or his blue-eyed palomino named Rocky, but they will always appreciate the honorable deed that we did."

Seymore smiled, and Rocky thought, "Life is exciting and good!"

Four

Blue-Eyed Palomino Facts

Blue-eyed palominos have a yellowish coat and a mane and tail that is silver or white. They are in the yellow dun group. Cowboys consider them as a separate group from the other duns.

A small amount of white on the face and legs is allowed by registries. Offspring do not necessarily show the same color pattern. The palomino is not considered a true breed, but there is a Palomino Horse Association. Palominos may also conform to the standards for the Arabian or the American quarter horse.

Palomino

Sometimes palominos and other duns have pink skin.

Pink-Skinned Palomino

Dappling is very common.

Dappled Palomino

Smutty palominos are yellow and black. Sometimes, even their tails are yellow and black.

Smutty Palomino

In America, the term *isabella* is used when referring to light cream-colored palominos without blue eyes. In Europe, this term is used to describe all palominos.

BEYOND "THE END"

In training horses, one trains himself.
Antoine De Pluvinet

WORD LIST
  blue-eyed palomino
  collar
  Tennessee Walking Horse
  slate grullo
  plowing
  reins
  turning millstones
  silver dun
  belly band
  dark buckskin
  loin strap
  towing barges
  traces
  haulage work

saddle
linebacked dun
girth
transportation
dappled palomino
bridle

From the word list above, write:

1. One word that names a breed of horse.

2. Five words that tell how horses were used in the early history of our country. What replaced the stagecoaches? What replaced the carriage and buggy? What replaced the wagons?

3. Eight words that name special tack needed for hitching up horses.

4. Six words that are color names for horses.

CURRICULUM CONNECTIONS

The Liberty Bell is real and represents America's freedom. Have you ever been to Philadelphia, Pennsylvania to see it?

The bell was cast in London. What materials were used to make the Liberty Bell? What words are written on the Liberty Bell?

The Declaration of Independence was written by our Founding Fathers to declare America's independence.

1. Who were the five men appointed to write the document?

2. How many revisions were made to their draft before it was signed?

3. Who was the first signer of the Declaration of Independence? Look at his signature!

Answers to these questions and the questions about the Liberty Bell can be found at <www.just4kidsmagazine.com/beacon4god/july4.html>.

Seymore Idunno said the Liberty Bell weighs 2,080 lbs. ("Ask Jeeves" at website <www.ask.com> why the abbreviation for *pound* is *lb.*)

1. How many pounds more than a short ton is 2,080 lbs.?

2. How many pounds less than a long ton is 2,080 lbs.?

PROJECT

Combine your math and artistic skills! Draw to scale and accurately color a picture (body, tail, and mane) of the horse that is featured in each book read in the Saddle Up Series. You could soon have sixty horses prancing around the walls of your classroom!
Learning + horses = FUN.

Look in your school library media center for books about how to draw a horse and the colors of horses. Don't forget the useful information in the last chapter of this book (Blue-eyed Palomino Facts) and the picture on the book cover for a shape and color guide.

HELPFUL HINTS AND WEBSITES
A horse is measured in hands. One hand equals four inches. Use a scale of 1" equals 1 hand.

Visit website <www.equisearch.com> to find a glossary of equine terms, information about tack and equipment, breeds, art and graphics, and more about horses. Learn more at <www.horse-country.com> and at <www.ansi.okstate.edu/breeds/horses/>. KidsClick! is a web search for kids by librarians. There are many interesting websites here. HORSES and HORSEMANSHIP are two of the more than 600 subjects. Visit <www.kidsclick.org>. Is your classroom beginning to look like the Rocking S Horse Ranch? Happy Trails to You!

ANSWERS (1. 70% copper, 25% tin and small amounts of lead, zinc, arsenic, gold, and silver. 2. "Proclaim liberty throughout all the land unto all the inhabitants thereof." 3. Thomas Jefferson, John Adams, Benjamin Franklin, Roger Sherman, and Robert R. Livingston. 4. 86 revisions. 5. John Hancock. 6. 80 lbs. more; 160 lbs. less.)